HEALING
——— IN THE ———
WAIT

Jannell Lankford

HEALING IN THE WAIT

HEALING IN THE WAIT
Janell Lankford

CONTENTS

PRAYER

Heavenly Father,

Consecrate my mind and my life so that I can live Holy unto you. Keep my mind and body that I may not sin against you. Although I am on this road temporarily single, I am desperate to keep from falling into temptation while I am waiting for my spouse. At night, when my body desires to go the wrong way, keep reminding me that this temple belongs to you. GOD if I happen to fall, please have mercy on me and forgive me. Take my hand and lead me back into your marvelous grace and into my righteous place, that I may not sin against you again. Your word says in Isaiah 26:3 You will keep in perfect and constant peace the mind that is steadfast and that is committed and focused on YOU—in both inclination and character. AMP

Peace is where I want to be with you while I wait on you for my imperfect, but perfect spouse.

Amen

A NOTE FROM JANNELL

If you find yourself in this book, I want you to hold on to it and become a better person as this book ministers to you. It is so hard when you want to please GOD, and yourself, but it is even harder when your heart desires to be right by GOD and you find yourself falling again, and again. As this was given to me by the Holy Spirit, I believed every word that was written, and I still believe every word that is written. But I noticed that it was hard for me at times to maintain these steps. I asked GOD daily to be with me and strengthen me. He knew I would make mistakes, but he wanted me to admit that I was not perfect, and if I had a heart to come back to him and repent unto him when I made mistakes. For some it is a walk in the park following God's word, but for others it is a struggle.

When this book was given to me it was instructions on how to live a righteous life while single. Then it spoke to me in my dating life. Now most people do not believe in dating unless you have a purpose, and I do too. But sometimes the person your dating has a different purpose than yours. In the beginning they seem to be speaking the same language, but later you find that their purpose does not align with yours. The truth of the matter is that it is alright, but you must learn from it, trust GOD, and get back up again because the right one is waiting. This book is not to encourage you to sin against GOD, but to live a life that is pleasing unto GOD. And if you find yourself knocked down, get up, dust yourself off, repent and move forward in GOD.

Jannell Lankford

CHAPTER 1

Acknowledging Your Faults

Ezra 10:11- So now confess your sins to the LORD, the GOD of our ancestor, and do what He demands. NLT

Acknowledging your faults is one of the hardest things to do. When you are a part of any relationship, and it doesn't work, don't spend half of your time talking about what the other person did wrong. Acknowledge what you did to contribute to your own hurt and allow GOD to fix you. No one is perfect, but we are perfect at seeing everyone else fault, but our own. When you cannot see your own fault GOD cannot fix you to be a better person for him, your family, or your future spouse.

Acknowledging your faults is sometimes going back to the person and asking for forgiveness, as well as forgiving those who have hurt you. What you are telling them is I made some mistakes when I was in a relationship with you and I apologize. No matter what kind of relationship it was, you just want to acknowledge your faults and be free. Your telling GOD I want your help in freeing me from not making the same faults again.

When you are dealing with deep rooted issues, that causes you to respond in a manner that does not please God, confess it unto GOD, because confession is good for the soul. Confession releases you from deep rooted strongholds, and it allows GOD to come and take over in your life. GOD wants to be glorified in everything that we do, so he wants to be the one that makes you over and cleanses you from the inside, but the only way he can do that is if you allow him to. One thing I love about GOD is, he is a gentleman, and he will not force himself into your life. He cannot change what you are dealing with if you do not allow him to.

PRAYER

Father GOD,

In the name of Jesus, you know my sins, all my wrongs, my faults, and the faults of others against me. As I lay them at the altar, I ask that you remove (state your faults/faults of others) that I may draw closer to you. Help me to remain humble, but also, strong so that my temple will not be easily tainted by my shortcomings. Help me to forgive those who have used me, and whom I feel may have caused me to act in a manner that was not pleasing unto you. In Jesus Name, Amen.

> Psalm 119: 29 Keep me from lying to myself; give me the privilege of knowing your instructions. NLT

CHAPTER 2

Get Rooted In The Word

Proverbs 12:3 Wickedness never brings stability, but the godly have deep roots. NLT

Rooted- To be established deeply and firmed, embedded, ingrained.

This one word has so much power when you take it seriously and fully understand its meaning. When you get "rooted" in the word of GOD, nothing can change your fruit. If you are not grounded, then sometimes all it takes is another life changing event to knock you off your feet and leave you feeling defeated. Let's be real. Being single and being rooted in the word is not what most believers want to do. Most of us have our own way of doing things and we want to be involved in relationships. However, the word of GOD requires us to do things differently. GOD's word requires us to search to find out about ourselves, our future, our spouses, and about our own children.

Spending time in the word gives GOD an opportunity to speak directly to us concerning how to be good stewards over our finances, how to raise our children, how to be a godly wife or husband, and how the two will function in ministry as one. Spending time with GOD in his word, is the best place for us. We will learn so much about ourselves, who you are in GOD, what a true husband/wife is, how to be a husband/wife, and what to expect of your wife/husband.

Applying the word also helps to bring order in your home. As a single parent, you will learn how to raise your children to be disciples of Christ and children of integrity...children of GOD. It will teach you that we are equal in the eyes of GOD and that you do not have to be their only parent. All things concerning and pertaining to them, you need to speak to their FATHER in heaven. Although they may not like it, it is the word and its right. It will teach you how to love as GOD loves and to not be so hard on them. It will teach you how to forgive yourself when you have done wrong, how to handle people correctly, how to manage your time and money, even how to pick friends. I could name so many, but those are some of the reasons why you would benefit from being rooted in God's word. GOD can and will teach you about himself, and about the one he created...YOU. If only you would commit to Him, put in time to build your character, and get in good standing with the Lord. How can you be faithful to your husband or wife if you cannot remain faithful to GOD? You are living in lust, dating anyone who asks, and entertaining people just because you are feeling lonely. The more time you spend doing those things, the less time you are spending in the word with GOD. It also causes an even longer time to prepare yourself for a godly marriage. If you are getting impatient then check to see where your roots are, and if you are truly ready for a Godly marriage.

PRAYER

Dear God,

As I searched your word, my heart was not with you. Although I was grounded, I was not truly rooted in you. Lord GOD I ask that you forgive me, and that I will be truly rooted in you and in your word as I submit to your will and your way of thinking. Help me to remember that you are the one who I need to be rooted in. Not in man, woman, or child, but only you. I ask that you uproot my roots from (Name it) and re-potter me back into you, the Potter. In Jesus Name, Amen

> Job 29:19-20 For I am like a tree whose roots reach the water, whose branches are refreshed with the dew. New honors are constantly bestowed on me, and my strength is continually renewed. NLT

CHAPTER 3

Mind Over Matter

Romans 8:6 So letting your sinful nature control your mind leads to death. But letting the Spirit controls your mind and leads to life and peace. NLT

The mind is a great place to begin when trying to decide who, what, where and when. When you begin to ask yourself those questions, things will begin to happen in your life. You must have a made-up mind that you will remain single until GOD sends your spouse, but more so, you will not give in to your matter. Webster's dictionary defines matter as, to be of importance; have significance. So, in this book, matter means to desire anyone or anything over The Father, The Son (Yahweh/Jesus Christ) and The Holy Spirit. It also means taking precedence over the things of GOD.

This was the most stressful topic for me because I was still wrestling with GOD about my husband, my flesh, and being lonely. I kept thinking GOD had forgotten all about me, that he was not hearing my prayers, and was not really concerned about me or my desires to be married again. I believed that if I just "stepped out" occasionally, I would be okay. GOD would forgive me then I could move past it and be delivered from it. I knew once I gave in to any of my matters that it would not be that easy for me to get over it because: 1. Now I know better 2. I understand how the spirits operate 3. If I am willing to be patient and obedient, GOD will send his chosen mate. Not (_____) hand-picked mate. Matthew 12:43-45 When an evil spirit leaves a person, it goes into the desert, seeking rest but finding none. Then it says, it will return to the person it came from. So it returns and finds its former home empty, swept, and in order. Then the spirit finds seven other spirits eviler than itself, and they all enter the person and live there. And so that person is worse off than before. That will be the experience of this evil generation. NLT

Start thinking about what happens when you pick your own mate, or when you do anything against the word of GOD. It could cause you to feel depressed and mad with yourself because "You should know better". You knew what was right, yet sometimes we fall short of the glory of Lord. It will get to a point when you get so tired of disappointing him, and tired of crying over the same things. James 4:17 So any person who knows what is right to do but does not do it, to him it is sin. AMP

Who would be there to pick up the pieces of your broken spirit and broken heart? GOD! Where would you go to escape from the mess you created? Back into the arms of GOD! Leaving the city that you have sinned in does not cause the sin to go away. Only a true heart of repentance, willingness, and a made-up mind not to do it again will cause it to stop. Once you have made up your mind that you are going to do right by GOD, it is hard to fall and not feel the urgency to repent and get back in his grace. You are to be very mindful how you act and respond to people. It is hard fighting against the matter that you once were so close with and you two did whatever you wanted to do. Sometimes you may give into your matter, but do not stay in your matter, and allow it to consume you to the place, that you are not able to get out of it, and back into the presents of GOD. You do not know when you will ever get married if you keep doing things at your own rate, rather than the Lord's. You could have been married a long time ago, but it would not have been a God-led marriage. It would have brought on more chaos rather than joy, excitement, and true love learning that in marriage there will be trials and tribulations.

Without GOD in the midst, your relationship will be the same mess you two had before the marriage. You will carry someone's last name (or have given someone your last name) that GOD had no intention on you being with. Then you will start questioning GOD about your failing marriage when all you had to do was seek him in the beginning. That is one reason why you should also seek Godly counseling before marriage. The marriage would have been denied or approved by GOD. It is not an easy process to have your mind renewed and to be led by GOD. Your mind has steered you into directions that you thought were God-led, or situations that you thought were God sent. Yet, even in process there is a point where you get stuck.

You cannot remove yourself from the situation, or it has become a repeating cycle for you. That is because your mind is influenced by your matter! Your matter is making the decisions, and your mind agrees because it does not remember how that decision did not work out last time. (Thinking that the outcome will be different) Now your matter is taking control and you are right back where you started from. Maybe with a different person, different reasoning, or different perspective about your decision. We think that if we do what we did last time to get out of the situation, whatever it may be, we will not get ourselves back into that place again. So, we get out of one situation, but back into that same situation with someone else. The people change, but the cycle never will until your mind is delivered and renewed. Romans 12:2 Don't copy the behavior and customs of this world, but let GOD transform you into a new person by changing the way you think. Then you will learn to know GOD's will for you, which is good and pleasing and perfect. NLT Isaiah 55: 8-9 My thoughts are nothing like your thoughts, says the LORD. And my ways are far beyond anything you could imagine. For just as the heavens are higher than the earth, so my ways are higher than your ways and thoughts higher than your thoughts. NLT

Once the word gets rooted and down into your soul, you will begin to think, speak, and live like Christ. Everything else will fail because nothing can defeat the word of GOD. If you are speaking it, believing it, and living it...GOD will change everything about you. So, whenever those matters arise, speak against them in the name of JESUS, and they will flee. A weak mind and a strong matter are what got you in those situations. Only a STRONG MIND will enable you to overcome "weak" matters. A Christ-like mind can get you out of the most impossible situations and circumstances. That is when you know your thinking is KINGDOM MINDED. When GOD has a plan for you, and you are operating in his will, you will receive the harvest. Whether it is marriage, a business, or whatever your heart desires. When you are obedient and submissive to GOD, He will bless you beyond measure.

PRAYER

Dear God,

As I prepare for transformation in my mind, to take on the mind of Christ, help me to be true to you. When I am weak, I am strong in you. You will see me through every trial and tribulation that may come up against me. Help me to remember that I am stronger than any matter that will tempt me to fall off the path that you have for me. Matter (name), I rebuke you in the name of Jesus, and cast you back into the pit of hell in which you came. You have no authority over my mind, body, or soul. This mind is in Christ! This body and soul belong to Christ Jesus! Because of the shed blood of Jesus and a renewed mind in Christ, I am made whole.

In Jesus Name, Amen

Psalms 94:19 When doubts filled my mind, our comfort gave me renewed hope and cheer. NLT

CHAPTER 4

Know How God Sees You

Romans 8:17 I am joint-heir with Christ. NLT

GOD sees you as a most valuable and precious jewel. You are priceless! No man or woman could ever love you as much as the FATHER does. Through all your mistakes, mishaps, and sin, he will never stop loving you. GOD will never put you down or make you feel less than. Begin to seek GOD and search his word to find out what the word says about you. Then start to believe God's word more than other people's opinions. Your goal is to become stronger, wiser, and smarter because of the word. GOD says........ (make it personal for you) *I am part of a chosen generation, a royal priest hood, a holy nation, a purchased people. 1 Peter 2:9*
*   I am a new creation in Christ. 2 Corinthians 5:17*
*   I can do all things through Christ Jesus.*
*   Philippians 4:13 I am an overcomer by the blood of the Lamb and the word of my testimony. Revelation 12:11*
I could go on and on about GOD and how his word says he sees us. GOD is greatness! GOD loved us so much that he sent his son to die for our sins. He came to earth in the form of a man, to experience everything that we would experience. He lived life without sin as an example to us all. Therefore, he can help us overcome any process without falling into sin. GOD does not see you as a mistake or a failure. Ladies he sees you as a beautiful Queen, and men he sees

you as King. He sees you as HIS precious and most valuable jewel on earth. You should never devalue yourself because of the opinion of a person. Never look at yourself as less than because you do not have the fancy car, or the big home, or you do not have degrees. All that does not determine how GOD sees you, but your true value is within him, not the earth. You are rich in Christ and beautiful and marvelous in his sight.

PRAYER

Father GOD,

In the name of Jesus... I ask that you open my eyes so that I may see me as you see me. Oh Lord help me to take the blinders off my eyes! Help me to stop dwelling on my past mistakes, and the negative words that others have spoken over me. Help me to believe only that which your word says about me. The truth is, I do not know all of what your word says about me. So, as I search your word, I ask that you reveal yourself to me. Show me myself as you see me. Father, I thank you for always seeing greatness in me. In Jesus Name, Amen.

Ephesians 1:7- I am forgiven of all my sins and washed in the blood.

CHAPTER 5

Damaged Goods Are Still Good

Philippians 2:13 For GOD is working in you, giving you the desire and the power to do what pleases him. NLT

We have all been through difficult times in our lives. Those things sometimes cause us to feel like we are unworthy for GOD and marriage. Honestly, we may not be, but because of grace and mercy, we are. For example, you go into the store for some canned goods. You go over to the shelf where they are stocked and pick up what you need. If you are not paying attention, you will pick up the ones that have all the dents. You may not notice the dents until you get home. You have the option of taking the canned goods back to the store for an exchange, but you realize the food you need is still on the inside of that dented can. So, you decide against taking that long trip back to the store and decide to keep the dented can. You eat it and enjoy it because nothing was different about the taste. The one and only difference was the dent on the outside appearance of the can. Sometimes our "outside appearances" may lead us into thinking that we are not good enough for others. Outer appearances are the experiences that we wear on us...our dents.

Our dents come from the different hurts, ups and downs, or any trials and tribulations that we have experienced. We began to see ourselves in a bad way, so we think other people see us in that same way. Most people cannot really see your dents. All they see is what is on the inside of us, which is joy, peace, happiness, love, Christ, and The Holy Spirit. The things you have experienced in life or in relationships, does not dictate who you are or what you are entitled to! Jeremiah 1:5 Before I formed you in the womb, I knew you and approved of you as My chosen instruments, and before you were born, I consecrated you to myself as my own, I have appointed you as a prophet to the nations. AMP.

GOD knew you before he formed you in your mother's womb. He knew that you would go through things that would bring you to your knees and make you feel unworthy. He needed you down in that place so that he could come in and repair your dents. Then he could begin to remind you of who you are. Although you may see yourself as damaged goods, God sees you as the best. Your spouse will look at all your dents and appreciate each one of them, and he/she will love you unconditionally, just as GOD does. Each dent that you carry, brings forth experiences, and revelation about things. It causes you to think before you decide but consult the FATHER before you say I DO.

PRAYER

Dear God,

I have caused/allowed so many situations and circumstances to become dents in my life. Those dents have affected my outer appearance and caused me not to see myself as you do. Father, I asked that you remove each dent out of my life. Although the repair process may hurt, I know that it is all for my good. Please do not allow me to be so focused on my dents that I miss the person whom you have chosen for me. Also, help me to notice the repaired area once you have removed the dents. God, I need you to help me to remain strong in you, and to remember that through all my experiences, you have always kept me.

In Jesus Name, Amen

> Romans 8:37 I am more than a conqueror through Him who loves me. NLT

CHAPTER 6

Learn Your Self-Worth

Mark 8:37 Is anything worth more than your
soul? NLT

A great majority of us spend our entire lives waiting for people to show us who we are to them, how much we mean to them, and what we must do to please them. Their approval makes us feel so special, as if their approval comes from GOD himself. We start thinking that nothing can destroy our feelings or the relationship that we have built with that person. Until that person tells us that they are not happy with something we did or did not say or do, or how we may have handled a situation our own way instead of theirs. Now we begin to feel less valuable because the person whom we love so much has become unhappy with us. Oftentimes we do not understand exactly why they are unhappy or unsatisfied, but since they have confessed it, we cannot handle it.

GOD chose us to do mighty things. So, when the wind blows, rain and storms come, we must stand in GOD. By faith, we must allow GOD to take us through it all. No matter what your past told you, your salvation speaks much louder. Family and friends know of your past, but they cannot even imagine your future. Which future is even brighter than your present? You must remember we are valuable! God sent his only son to die for us! You must take his death personally and as a reminder that you are valued, and you are worthy

24

of his unconditional love. Regardless of man or woman, family, or friends, you do not have to be who anyone wants you to be, to be happy. Be who God wants you to be in him, and always be happy. When you learn how valuable you are, you will not be moved by what others say or think about you. Vengeance is the Lord's, and he will deal with others accordingly.

Question: How does one learn their value?

Romans 10:9-10 If you openly declare that Jesus is LORD and believe in your heart that God raised him from the dead, you will be saved. For it is by believing in your heart that you are made right with GOD, and it is by openly declaring your faith that you are saved.

Accepting JESUS as your LORD and Savior changes things about you, and who you are. His name validates who you are, and who you were once before does not matter anymore. You must take charge over your life, speak those things as though they are, and stand in GOD. Understand this, GOD makes nothing cheap and he does not spend time creating junk or messy art. You are pottered by the POTTER who took his time to create everything in you and about you, and when he blew the breath of life in you, he blew his plan, purpose, will, and spirit of himself into your body.

You began as a diamond in the ruff and once GOD finishes pressurizing you, you will be the most beautiful diamond on earth, and like any value thing you just cannot leave it sitting around, and on the hand or arms of folks who are so undeserving of you. Right now, you may not see yourself the way the LORD sees you but keep speaking the word of GOD over your life and watch GOD show up and show you who you are. How you see yourself is how everyone would see you, and no matter how much you speak over your life, or other people speak positively over your life, if you do not believe it then it will be nothing but spoken words unfulfilled.

Seeing yourself as the FATHER sees you is an amazing feeling. It does not make you conceited, boastful, or arrogant. It makes you confident in GOD which comes with humility and being humble. GOD can change the value of any person who is willing to see themselves destined for greatness in him and the kingdom. He knows the price he paid for you and once you receive and believe it was because of you he died then you will never know your true value. NO man or woman would lay down their life for you in the manner which he did. Because of JESUS, you should appreciate his words about you and walk in your awesomeness.

CHAPTER 6.1

Take Time To Get To Know Yourself

Ecclesiastes 7:22 For you know how often you yourself have cursed others. NLT

Getting to know yourself is the best way to get to know who you really are, and what you want for yourself. Oftentimes we become a part of who others say we are. We do things that other people say we should do. Or we act according to what others say is the right way to act. We respond to things, people, and life situations by the way we see our parents or someone else respond. To them it was okay, so to us it became okay. You must make the final decision to put yourself and those familiar responses behind you. It is your past. Ask yourself: Is this really who I am? Is this the way I want to be? Is this who I want to be? Is this where I want to be? (Mental stability)

Example: The judge says you are a felon. So, you start acting like a felon. Instead of looking to start your own business and furthering your education, you start selling drugs and committing robberies. Because of whom society says you are, you start believing the identity they created for you. Cannot get a good job, cannot live in a decent house, cannot drive a nice car, cannot get ahead. All because you feel stuck in a category, with a title that man has given you...not God.

You must begin taking time out for yourself, talking with yourself and GOD about making decisions that are pleasing, and benefit you, not other people. You have started communicating with the Father more about your life, your children's life if you have any, and what he has called you to do and be in ministry. Allow GOD to do a new thing in you, and GOD will begin saying YES! and Amen. He really desires to do something, powerful in your life, and just as the bible speaks of miracles and signs of deliverance, he wants you to receive yours. (Say I received mine). Amen GOD, Glory to your name. LORD I thank you for coming off your throne to come see about me. Be opened to try new things in GOD. It will give you a deeper love for GOD, and a different love for your children. He will allow you to see them as he created them, but how to love them, and how to love yourself. If you are expecting GOD to do great and mighty things in your life you must do things differently. Losing friends, and relationships is not the end of the world, it is GOD plan for the better.

This may not make sense with this topic but to spend time with GOD, you began to learn things that you thought you knew, but now how to apply it to your life to see the fulfillment of the LORD move in your life. I never understood why people that say they love you could do and say some of the cruelest things to you, then I learned it is not you who they are upset with. They may be upset with things not going right in their lives and are taking it out on you.

Learn your gift in GOD, how to use your gift, how to protect your heart, and your kids. Learn things to do to cause generational curses to fall off your life and your children. Take time to learn that the GREAT I AM, has and will always be with you. He is just waiting for you to say yes and give him your hand and your heart so he can teach you more about yourself, and him. We are created in his image and his likeness. When we become one with the FATHER, we embody how he responds to situations and the appropriate action to take.

When you begin to learn about yourself, and find faults that are displeasing to you, you create the atmosphere of wanting to change.

It will become your heart desires to keep searching yourself and learning more about you. You may find there are things that you like but would never expose yourself to because of the opinions of others. Just remember their opinions about your life do not matter.

For example: While learning yourself, you will learn that having sex is good, but having it with your husband or wife is better. You will begin to change your perspective about yourself and your temple that laying down with any person, or a person you are in a relationship is not pleasing, but it is not pleasing to GOD.

So, you begin to think "If I wait and don't have sex will I ever get married, because nowadays most people don't want to wait for marriage, and I don't want to be single forever". Remember obedience is better than sacrifice, and GOD knows what he is doing, just wait. When you are getting to know yourself, you begin to learn that you are valuable, and sacred. You become more conscious about yourself and what others think and say really does not matter. Take time getting to know yourself through the mind, and eyes of the Father, and you would also learn so much about who you are as a person. It takes time so start by not listening to people's opinion about you.

CHAPTER 6.2

Free Yourself From Yourself

John 8:36 So if the Son sets you free, you are truly free. NLT

As people, we tend to hold ourselves captive. We will not let go of the past, or even current hurts, failures, disappointments, or relationships. We tend to make it so hard for ourselves to move forward. We are caught up on the "what ifs", the "why's", the "who's" and the "I don't understand". Some things are not for you to understand at that time. They are in place to cause you to move forward in the things of Christ. When God has a plan for you, he does whatever it takes to move you out of any situation so that he can operate in your life without distraction.

For one to be free, you must be free from all the pain, mess, confusion, lack, misunderstandings, hurts and foolishness. Some of us think we are free when we are no longer in certain relationships. We believe that we are now free from that person, so we are now free to move on to the next. We are so wrong! We are not actually free from that person until our heart is free from them. Moving on into another relationship should not even be an option when the door to the first relationship has not been closed.

Jeremiah 17:10 But I, the LORD, search all hearts and examine secret motives. I give all

30

people their due rewards, according to what
their actions deserve. NLT

When you allow your heart to hold onto things, people, events, or circumstances, it causes you to be hindered. How can God send the one He's chosen for you if you are still holding on to someone else? Why do we choose to stay mad or hold on to hurt from the past? If God decided to send that special mate, he/she would never experience a true love from us. They would not be able to reach that special place in your heart because the moment they do something "suspicious" or like something you have experienced, you will begin to treat them like the enemy.

We may have to take a disappointment or loss from what we wanted, but our FATHER knows best. When praying and asking God if that is the man or woman you are dating not in his will for your life, God will show you each time. You must know God has a mate for you somewhere. Settling and compromising is not an option anymore, but patience and his timing is.

Sometimes we love a particular person so much that we begin to look for them, or certain characteristics of them, in other people. We constantly compare everyone to that one person, even if it is unintentional. A lot of situations in your life could have been avoided if you took the time to free yourself from your last relationship, and free yourself from yourself by forgiving yourself. Allow God to heal all your wounds. Then you will begin to see each person for who they are, not who you desire them to be.

When you are not free, you tend to do the same things you have done before salvation. You still think it is okay to have sex with someone because you are in a "relationship". You do not take them to meet your Pastor, and it does not matter to you whether they attend church. You still act the same and think the same, which causes you to have the same responses. Just know, that who the Son sets free is truly free indeed! You are free from all negative thoughts of yourself and your past. You are free from thoughts and opinions of others and how they perceive you. You are free from bondage. You must see yourself as God sees you. Know and understand your self-worth and do not settle. Spend time reflecting on the Word of God and free your mind from self-destruction. Take hold of the promises of GOD and lose yourself from yourself from him/her that holds you in a still position. Beginning in that position will cause a delay in who GOD has destined for you to be with because you are waiting for a change or a move of GOD when GOD is showing you and telling you that he/she is not the one.

You cannot expect for GOD to show up when your heart's not in the right place, and your mind. Your mind says I want to be free; your prayer says the same thing, but your heart says I want who I want. When the heart wants what it wants it will not allow anyone to approach you because it deflects the spiritual energy you need and reflects the energy you do not need.

> Psalm 51:10 Create in me a clean heart, O GOD and renew a right and steadfast spirit within me. AMP

Oh! gracious GOD,

Help me to learn myself worth in you GOD, do not allow me to depreciate myself because I do not see me as value to any man/woman, let alone to myself. Help me to be confident in you LORD that I will know that I am worth the death of your son Jesus. God teach me to be what you have called me to be for the work of your kingdom, and for my spouse. I have spent so much of my life living for people and doing things the way other people say I should have done things and lost who I was, as a person, a mother, a father, husband, wife, a friend, sister, brother, aunt, uncle. (read what applies) God I have an idea of who I am, but I do not know if it is who you say I am. God help me get to know you better, that I may learn through you who I am. Your ways are not my ways, your thoughts are not my thoughts. I know longer want to be who I thought I was, and who people say I am. I do not want to keep pretending and being unhappy within myself, so that others may be happy. I want to be free to be who I am in Christ Jesus. My inner person longs to be free, free Lord, your word says who the Son set free is free indeed. Change me oh LORD and wash me new in you. Today I take on the mind of Christ that my mind may be renewed. I pray that I will see myself as you see me...victorious. I am free from my sins and myself. I surrender all my pain, hurt, guilt, shame, frustration, anger, depression, lack, suicide thoughts, feelings of worthlessness and pity. I am putting on the yoke of Christ because it is lighter, and with it comes freedom, joy, peace, love, happiness, understanding and confidence. I am assured that I am greater than any man's validation of me, and I am stomping on the devil's head. I AM VICTORIOUS! I am choosing to be free in you. I know your plans are greater than I can imagine. I also know that my mate will be great for me too.
God Thank you.
In Jesus Name, Amen

Galatians 5:1 Christ has truly set us free. Now make sure that you stay free, and do not get tied up again in slavery to the law.

Roman 13:14 Cloth yourself with the presence of the LORD Jesus Christ. And do not let yourself think about ways to indulge your evil desires.

Acts 20:24 My life is worth nothing to me unless I finish the work assigned to me.

CHAPTER 7

Take Time To Heal

Psalms 147:3 He heals the brokenhearted and bandages their wounds. NLT

Healing is a process. It takes time to heal from all the hurt and pain you have endured over the years. You cannot choose how long your healing will take. Just be willing to go through the healing process. Take as much time as need so that you can be who GOD has called you to be. Be everything in him that he needs you to be. God cannot use a broken vessel. He sees so much more in you than brokenness. God does not want you to lose your anointing because you will not let go. Healing can be so hard and so uncomfortable. Sometimes it may seem easier just to stay in that broken place because you do not want to experience that pain again. Come out! Coming out of your brokenness is the only way God can heal you.

Dealing with whatever causes you to become broken allows you to put it aside as if it never happened. Healing comes from confronting it, accepting that it was wrong, and forgiving the person(s) who caused the brokenness. God wants to restore you! He is an amazing GOD, and only he can do the impossible. If you thought you could never be healed from the mess of your past, watch God show you otherwise. After healing you will be able to get to a place where you will trust your future husband or wife. When you are not fully healed, you are unable to trust anyone. You may want to trust, and your acting skills may be great to where you can pretend to trust, but you really do not. You are even treating God like a man because you are not really trusting him. But God is not like man that he will lie, or cause hurt to your life and soul. When you carry a burden for twenty- three years you must ask, "do I still want to carry this burden, or do I want God's healing touch"? Self-healing can be smoking marijuana, having sex with any man or woman, being abused mentally, emotionally, sexually, physically, and financially, thinking you are a homosexual, clubbing and finding comfort in anyone who wants you. You are damaging yourself from the inside out. When you allow God to come in and restore everything that was broken within you, to heal you and make you whole again, you become a much better person, and free. Others will remember your name, but they will hardly recognize God's new creation...You.

It is important that you take the time and allow God to heal you from your past. Not just old relationships, but from friendships, failures, and even family issues. While you're waiting on God to send your mate, allow him to do whatever he needs to do in you. In time, God will heal your broken heart. He will cause you to open your heart to not only love him more, but also yourself. You will be open to whomever it is that God has for you and be able to truly love that person. True healing comes when you don't go back to the place that caused the pain mentally, physically, emotionally, or spiritually. You will be tested in the areas of your healing just to see if you believed that you were healed or just to see how you would respond, but when you begin to speak life, over the situation and pray about then GOD knows he is in control and he will keep working miracles in your life.

PRAYER

Dear God,

I am in this healing process with you, please work on me from the inside out so that I will not bring any mess from my past into my future relationships. Thank you, GOD, for healing me and freeing my heart from spiritual soul ties that were not conducive for me or my life. As you continue to heal me, I thank you for your unconditional love, support and understanding. Even more so, for always thinking of me when I was not thinking of myself. Thank you for wanting the best for me when I had no hope for myself and my family. Thanks for loving me.
In Jesus Name,
Amen

1 Corinthians 12:9 The same Spirit gives great faith to another, and to someone else the one Spirit gives the gift of healing. NLT

CHAPTER 8

Seek Godly Counsel

Proverbs 19:20 Get all the advice and instruction you, can so you will be wise the rest of your life. NLT

This topic is the hardest part for most people because no one wants anyone to tell them who they can and cannot date. When it comes to dating, we think we have it all figured out and we know who is best for us, and what is best for us, so we do not bring that topic of dating to the forefront to our Pastors. Dating to us seems to be our personal life and our Pastors should not really have a say so to who we are dating, but they do. Sharing who you are dating to your Pastor holds you accountable to living right before GOD and doing things in order. For those who do not have a Pastor, you should find a church home for every area in your life, so GOD is able to speak to you directly about the areas in your life that are lacking. For those who do not have that relationship with their Pastor, seek an Elder in your church with wisdom, someone whom you can trust, who loves, GOD and can lead you in the right direction.

This portion I love because I am guilty of not wanting to share my personal life with anyone let alone my Pastor. But GOD set it up that she and I would have a relationship. Before I became a member of my new church, I never really had anyone spiritual to talk to, so I would seek GOD and do what I thought I heard him say. Now if

I followed all directions given then it went well, but if I followed some of the directions and add flesh it would fail. When I became a member of NLKC GOD exposed me to a woman who cared about me, my children, and the wellbeing of my life. It was through her teaching that GOD polished me. He knew I still was not ready to talk to her, so he used her messages to talk to me. Then her and I had our first one on one. To my amazement she did a one on one I never had done before. My Pastor was able to pour into my life all I needed spiritual, and natural. Never judging me, she embraced me and loved me, taught me, and rebuked me if needed. This allowed me to share with her about dating and my past relationships. She then would guide me spiritually with what I needed, and naturally understand what I was going through. But she always reminded me to stand on the word of GOD and in due season when the time was right, GOD would send a GODLY husband to me and my children. But more so right now GOD needed my full undivided attention to work on me, and she was right and listening to her has helped me become a much better person, for myself, my children, and my future husband, but more so for ministry.

A real man or woman of God will always protect you from a person that is sent to destroy you and the well-being of your children if you have any. A man or woman of GOD can see things that you may not be able to see in a person, so when you are confiding in them it is only to help guide you in making a decision that will bring joy, and prosperity in your life. Who wants a person that is always unhappy, insecure, a cheater, a liar; no one does? Sometimes your mind is clouded with that person and those things you cannot see, or you just do not see, and your Pastor is there to help bring light to dark situations.

You must be mindful because there are some Pastors that are not truly living for GOD; they prey on the single women, and men of the church to get them to fall in their lies and deceits, which cause people to lose hope and faith in GOD, but the body of Christ. You must be under a ministry that you see GOD operating in, meaning you see more marriages than divorces. You must watch the marriage of your Pastor and the First Lady, or her Husband. That alone will speak value about their marriage, and their union with GOD. Some Pastors are good at faking a happy home, but it will not be long before GOD exposes them to their congregation. The enemy has a way of hiding the truth from the blind, but GOD will open the eyes of the believer to see what they need to see so they can leave and be in a ministry that will teach and groom them for the kingdom and their spouse. The truth of the matter is when a man or woman of GOD are truly in love with GOD, their heart is always about pleasing GOD and the people of GOD. He or she would never intentionally hurt someone. Let alone the people they believe GOD has sent to them to assist them in ministry. Taking the time to get to know your man or woman of GOD says a lot about you and your well-being for yourself and your family. They are not just there to preach the gospel to you, or treat you as the FATHER would, they are the example of whom Jesus was to the disciples and the people that he taught. Although everyone did not like him let alone understand him, they respected and loved Jesus' ministry, and many were healed and delivered because he followed GOD and obeyed. That should be your Pastor, and if it is not you should ask GOD to place you in a church to get what you need for ministry, for your future, and for your children.

PRAYER

Dear Heavenly Father,

Help me to seek wise and GODLY counsel while I wait for the man or woman of GOD you have for me. Help me not to fall into temptation but be strong in you. Lord teach me to have an ear to hear what the Holy Spirit has to say to me, while you use the man or woman of GOD to counsel me. Help me to be strong in you when I feel like giving up. Bless the one who I seek for wisdom.
Jesus Name,
Amen

Job 22:18 "Yet He filled their houses with good things; But the counsel of the wicked and ungodly is far from me". AMP

CHAPTER 9

L.I.I (Live In Integrity)

Job 8:20 "Behold, God will not reject a man of integrity, nor will He strengthen or support evildoers. AMP

Websites define integrity as the quality of being honest and having strong moral principles; moral uprightness; the state of being whole and undivided.

The truth of L.I.I (Living in Integrity) is it is an amazing thing when you stand in it and you know your worth and your value, and yet you refuse to compromise. When you become a new person in Christ all things old have passed away, now all things are new to you. When you have a made-up mind and you choose to follow Christ and surrender your bad habits and old ways of thinking, you give GOD room to move in your life, to train and prepare you to be a wife or husband. GOD said my ways are not your ways and my thoughts are not your thoughts. That means he is always thinking beyond what you can imagine. When you are in GOD everything about you changes.

How you respond to people, your reactions to conversations that are not godly, your dress code changes, the way you think. You have now become a person who once did a thing you do not do any more especially for the name of Love for a man or woman. You must be unmovable and unshakable with this walk in Christ. I am not saying do not date, but you and GOD know you if dating is going to cause you in 90 days to be on your back then leave it alone until you are strong enough in the LORD to date.

If dating for you causes you to start missing church, fornicate, not actively being involved in ministry, unable to pay your tithes or give because your money was spent on that person rather than GOD house, hold your course and allow GOD to pick your mate. GOD said only what you do for his house will last. Seek the Kingdom of GOD and these things would be added unto you, besides GOD knows your desire to be married, and out the single pool, and he will bring you out just be patient. Stand in FAITH and INTEGRITY until he/ she comes.

Also, if that person has an issue with your Pastor and church then you need to leave it alone because GOD does not bring confusion. If he or she has their own church meet with your Pastor and discuss with him or her about you two visiting one another church. That goes back to the last chapter: it holds you accountable for your actions and speaks value to you, but also lets GOD know that you honor and respect your Pastor who he has given to you. Invite them to your church. Bring them to meet the woman or man of GOD that may influence you as your Pastor if they are already active in ministry and are involved in church. Women, if he is not involved in a church or local ministry invite him. Men, if you are not in a church it is okay to follow her to become what GOD has called you to be.

Now if you catch yourself slipping or drifting from the things of GOD and no longer doing the things you were once doing before repenting and get back in the boat. The word of GOD says Proverbs 24:16 For a just man falleth seven times, and riseth up again, but the wicked shall fall into mischief. KJV

In other words, GOD knows no one is perfect and that you may make some mistakes along this walk but get back up, do not sit idle in sin, and continue doing it because now it is not a mistake it is you wanting to be there. You must know that you belong to GOD and that no matter what, you will not give into the temptation of the flesh. 1 John 4:4 Dear children, you belong to God. You have not accepted the teachings of the false prophets. That is because the

One who is in you is more powerful than the one who is in the world. NIVR

When it gets lonely and you are ready to date and want to spend some adult time with someone of the opposite sex, or when you are dating, and you have been dating for a while and sex is the topic more than GOD this scripture helps Psalm 121:1-3 look up to the hills. Where does my help come from? 2My help comes from the Lord. He is the Maker of heaven and earth. 3He will not let your foot slip. He who watches over you will not get tired. NIV

GOD would bring you out of any situation that does not please him, because you bring glory to the FATHER when you honor him and live right and for him.

PRAYER

Heavenly Father,

Oh, gracious GOD help me to find integrity in you, and that I may live a life that is Holy and acceptable unto you. LORD pleasing you is more important than pleasing man. If I fall short please forgive me Father and teach me your way of living, thinking, and responding to the cares of this world. Help me when I am weak to look to you for strength and not man. Continue to be with me as your word says you will never leave me nor forsake me, thank you LORD that your thoughts are higher than my thoughts and your ways are not my ways. Thank you for the blood of Yahuwah (Jesus).

In Jesus Name
Amen

Psalm 25:21 Let integrity and uprightness protect me, For I wait [expectantly] for You. AMP

CHAPTER 10

Grow From Your Past Relationship

JOB 17:9 Nevertheless the righteous will hold to his ways, and he who has clean hands will grow stronger and stronger. NASB

Every relationship has its ups and downs and from each relationship you have taken something from it, whether it is happiness, sadness, trust, insecurities, pain, rejection, guilt, or shame. Some things were taken away or left with you. The sad part is you took a piece of your past relationship with you into another relationship. You never took the time to grow from the relationship because you keep jumping from one ship to another hoping this relationship would fix what broke you down or add something more than the previous relationship. No more do you need to keep going through all that. STOP taking yourself through that. Take a moment to breathe, scream, cry, eat, exercise, pray but DO NOT GO through it again. GROW from it.

Take all your past relationships, and experiences and grow from it to become a better, stronger, healthier, and loving person. Despite how he or she has treated you or you treated them, ask for their forgiveness, and ask to be forgiven so GOD can begin to heal you. Forgiveness is never really for the other person but for you. Allow

GOD to take the broken pieces of your heart and bring forth a masterful transformation.

Do not play the victim.

It is hard playing the victim when you are trying to be in other relationships and move past the last relationship. Acting like the victim makes it hard to love or be loved. You will just keep taking and rolling all your issues and everything else into another relationship. Never taking the time to STOP and GROW.

I remember reading in Matthew 6:15 But if you do not forgive others [nurturing your hurt and anger with the result that it interferes with your relationship with God], then your Father will not forgive your trespasses. AMP

Now you must begin forgiving, but also forgive everyone you thought had caused you some type of destruction in your life. I am not just talking about forgiving him or her, but your parents, friends, Pastors, leaders, ex boyfriends, whomever it takes for you to be forgiven by the Father. When it sinks in, it makes it much clearer to love, and forgive.

Relationships of any kind can break you down, but a relationship in GOD will take all that mess and cause you to grow into a person that you never knew existed. When you take the time to grow, you take the time to get to know you and grow into the person of GOD not man.

I have been dating since I was 12 years old off and on until I was 35. For 23 years of my life, I have been with someone. Not all were bad nor good, but I have had some that made me feel worthless, trashy, stupid, dumb, nasty etc. Some brought joy, and money. Through all those relationships I had been labeled by each man. Each one had attached themselves to me. I moved on hoping that the new one could remove the label from the old one, but they could not; they just kept adding up.

I got into this place of trying to find myself, but instead I found GOD. I am not saying it was an easy transition from my own way of doing things to the way of GOD, but I had to try him. I had tried everyone else. Their way was messy. Although I messed up several times, GOD has always forgiven me, but gave me wisdom and instructions on how not to be in that state again. He taught me what to look for in people that I was meeting. GOD had begun removing people from my life so that his will could be done in my life. I had begun growing in GOD that I may be able to teach his word, encourage others and to write this book. I grew up in GOD, but I also grew up in my mind.

Change the way you think, how you respond to every man or woman that thinks you are attractive or want to date you. Begin to ask questions you would not normally have asked in your past relationships: What is marriage all about? What do you want for yourself? How do you find out who a man or woman truly is?

Forgive yourself for bad choices you have made. If you know that you want to be married or get remarried again you must grow from your past relationship. Do not allow them to hinder you from being who GOD has called you to be and when it is time then GOD will send him or her to you.

We know that there is more to life, than worrying about a man or woman, who loves you, or whether to forgive and let go or hold on and be miserable. You cannot hold on and you cannot be miserable. You can cause someone else's life misery because you cannot get it together. You must get to that point in life that you begin to love you. When you get to the place in your life when loving yourself and GOD more than the person or peoples who have betrayed you, you will be much happier.

Is it hard? Yes. Will you get lonely? Yes. Will you miss dating? Yes. It is only by the word of GOD that you will be able to stand. Ask GOD himself to fill you up with the Holy Spirit so you will not focus on being single. Wherever you find yourself in a relationship grow from what you have been through or are currently going through and become victorious and not the victim. Some relationships will leave you feeling like a victim, but how long you choose to remain a victim is up to you. I am not saying that you will forget it, or get over it overnight, but when you put your trust and faith in the LORD Almighty you will never fail, but YOU WILL ALWAYS WIN.

Heavenly Father,

You know my weakness and my strengths, and you know my struggles that I fight with every day to grow and be strong in you. Help me Oh Lord to be what you have ordained me to be from the foundation of the Earth. Help me to find strength in your word and forgiveness in my heart. Anything that is in me that is not like you please remove it. Help me to grow in the things of Christ and not flesh. Teach me Oh, Lord the way of Christ and not self, help me to be selfless as you are to be overcome and be victorious in you.
In Jesus Name
Amen

Galatians 6:9 Let us not grow weary or become discouraged in doing good, for at the proper time, we will reap if we do not give up. AMP

CHAPTER 11

Refuse To Go Back

Proverbs 29:1 He who hardens his neck and refuses instructions after beginning often reproved (corrected, criticized), will suddenly be broken beyond repairs. AMP

Y ou must remember what you have been through in your past relationships and refuse to go back through it again. You must begin to see some value in yourself, for your husband/ wife to see value in you. People say you tend to attract people that are like minded. I believe our spirit tends to let off an aura that attracts us to the same type of person who we dealt with or had some type of relationship with and we find ourselves back in the same relationship status. This is not just for dating this for any type of relationship, friendships, family ship etc. You can want a friendship with certain people, and they may not be GOD's best for you and where he is trying to take you and you must let them.

I had some friends in middle school that I thought were so close and that we will remain friends from high school, to college, to raising our kids together, and that never happened. I asked GOD why. He said because where I am positioning you in life, they are not ready to go where you are going, they are not willing to sacrifice so much as you are, their things in their life that they are ready to let go. I must use you to show them who I AM and when they need me

50

then they will seek me. At the time it never made sense to me, and some days it still does not make sense to me, but I watch how GOD uses me to encourage them, speak a word in their life, and pray for them. I would have never been able to do that if I were not disconnected from them. I am not saying their lives are bad, or we were always getting in trouble, but what I am saying is when GOD wants to use us, he is going to use you whether you are ready or not he will make you ready. It is a blessing to be able to pour back in the lives of so many people, when they knew how you used to be and how you have changed.

When you let people go naturally from your life, you also have let them go spiritually, because if not you find yourself picking up the same type of people that GOD just removed out of your life. You must value yourself as a person and see yourself how GOD sees you, and not compromise yourself and your well- being for anyone. It does not matter who they are, your parents, siblings, cousins, aunts, uncle, friend, girlfriend, boyfriend do not allow people to treat you any kind of way and think it is alright. Especially when you have been through so much with people, and GOD knows your pain that person or persons may have caused you. You must remember those sleepiness nights, those crying nights, that never ending pain. The days and nights when you could not eat, the days where you thought about suicide, or you felt worthless. The nights you cried out to GOD and seemed as if he never heard your cry and felt your pain. You cried so much that your face was swollen for days. And if you meet someone who has some of the characteristics of a person that has caused some of that pain and hurt you can refuse that relationship too, because guess what it is the same spirit different person. When you have made up in your mind, that I LOVE ME MORE and refuse to go back, then you will start to see positive things coming to you that were not there before.

The enemy knows what you been through and he wants to diffuse GOD's blessing as much as possible. He wants you to think that GOD does not hear your prayer, or he does not care about you, that is why the same people or people of like spirits keep entering your life, but the word says Proverbs 3:6 In all your ways know and recognize Him, and He will make your path straight and smooth (removing obstacles that block your way). AMP

Anyone that causes a blockage in your life GOD wants to remove it, but you must be willing to allow GOD to do just that, remove them. You are going to have some ups and downs with people that you love that does not mean cutting them out of your life. I am speaking of those that cause you more grief, pain, heartache than joy, peace, happiness. I am speaking of that friend who never shows up for any of your events, and never invites you to theirs. I am speaking of that cousin that calls you when they are going through something but never answers for you. I am speaking of that one you would give your last dime to, but never have it when you need it. I am speaking of that mate that is only affectionate when he/ she wants some things. I am speaking of that person that shut you out because they do not really want you there, but they know that there is a call on your life and when you rise, they do not want you to rise without them. That friend or loved one who is praying on your downfall you know this by the way they treat you. Once GOD removes them, REFUSE to go back to anything toxic. You can still love them, but you cannot keep them around you, they are too toxic for you.

Sometimes the mate that GOD is trying to get to you, cannot come because of those that are attached to you and because GOD is a spirit, he will not bring his spirit in a toxic environment and that is why you keep missing your mate because you are not refusing the bad mates or spirits. When GOD's love hits you it overcomes everything, but when you have people around that is always negative your love will never last because you are going to want to listen to everyone's opinion and ask everyone what they think of your mate. You want to please everyone. But if you are not pleasing to GOD then you are not pleasing anyone. It is GOD that brings forth unions that are unbreakable, unmovable, unshakable not man.

An environment that causes so much grief and headache will cause your relationship to spiral downward, because you will spend so much time trying to make one another feel better that you never really build trust, getting to know one another.

PRAYER

God,

There is something that I am currently going through, and it is hard for me to overcome. I have some past things I have refused to let go, and I want to let them go. I refuse to fall back into past relationships that will block you from moving in my life. Help me to be strong in you so that I will not look back, and that I will not be put in relationships that will remind me of my past ship. Thank you for protecting me from my past, forgive me for my unwillingness to let go.

Amen

Isaiah 7:20 If you refuse and rebel, you shall be devoured by the sword. For the mouth of the LORD has spoken. NKJV

CHAPTER 12

The Pattern Never Changes

Proverbs 4:14 Do not enter the path of the
wicked, and do not go the way of evil men.
AMP

The pattern of men or women never changes when you are
waiting for GOD to send your future husband or wife. In
this chapter you must understand that the enemy hears and
understand your prayer when you are not praying in your heavenly
language. As bad as you want to be a wife or a husband you must pay
close attention to the person that you are dating. The pattern of the
serpent never changes but the appearance of him does and although
he or she may not look like the person you once dated before or
sound like that person, watch the behavior of that person.

When you are dating someone new, they always make themselves sound better than any person that you have dated before, and
they would even do things in the beginning to make sure that they
are different then the person you date. They want to be able to build
trust with you or be intimate with you. They want you to be able
to see them as that special someone. These people are not aware
that they are being used to be a distraction to you, to make you fall
while you are keeping yourself close to God. These people make you
believe their lies as they are telling them. They do not know that they
are lying because they believe themselves. They cannot control who

they are; they know that you are a part of their assignment as you are GOD's assignment.

The pattern of an ungodly man never changes with the words he speaks out of his mouth, let alone his actions towards you. Some will wine & dine you, buy gifts, pray with you, and promise to come to church. Others will come to church with you and never once change their mind about waiting for marriage. If the Holy Spirit has already told you what it was, he also would show you the patterns, conversations, action when they are in your presence, and their walk with Christ. Although I have no room to judge anyone, walk with Christ but I do know 2 Corinthians 6:14 Do not be yoked together with unbelievers. For what do righteousness and wickedness have in common? Or what fellowship can light have with darkness? NIV

Sometimes where others are in their walk, you cannot wait for them to catch up with you. They are not ready to be committed to the way of Christ. They would keep making excuses as to why they have not fully come into the house of GOD and allow him to cleanse and deliver them from mess. They say they love GOD, but they do not go to church, because the Pastor house is bigger than mine, and the Pastor stealing the church money and the people are fake and every excuse they may have. But I am not one for many excuses. I know we all have been hurt by people, but what do people have to do with GOD dealing with you? People do not like to be judged, but they find it easy to judge other people. When you start speaking about the people of GOD and the man or woman of GOD not only are you judging, but you are assuming. As I tell them GOD is soon to return and he will deal with each one accordingly. So, while you are worried about them you need to work on your own salvation.

You must be mindful when you are dating when you see that person is starting to respond, or act like someone from a previous relationship. You must question their motives and walk away. Pray that GOD shows you who they are so that you are not caught up in someone GOD never intended to be in your life, and do not be so quick to jump into a relationship to have someone. I am not saying do not date him/ her. I mean take your time to get to know that person spiritually, emotionally, socially, and mentally. That does not mean you have to commit to that person as girlfriend or boyfriend it means until you know who they are to you, you want to be friends and if you are for him/her than you are and if you are not then you are not, and that is alright. You have so much to look forward to in a marriage. Running off with the first person that is not in GOD'S will, will lead you to a divorce.

PRAYER

Heavenly father,

I may not always get it right the first time, but rest assured I am willing to give it all I got until I get it right every time. I do not want to fall back into habits and old ways just to be in a relationship with someone. I do not want to be fearful of dating. I just want to be right with you. I want you to be in my decision making because my past decisions have brought me to a place of anger, hurt, confusion, and bitterness, and I do not want to be like that anymore. Open my eyes that I may see the patterns of the enemy trying to work himself back in my life through people. Open my eyes that I may see darkness as he tries to approach me with lies, and fake concern that will try to make me mate with him, that I may fall short of your glory. Help me Oh! Lord to expose him/her until my mate arrives. GOD, I know the process will be hard, but I know you have the final say so, in you I live, move, and have my beginning, and I will always WIN.
Amen

Ephesians 4:27 Do not give the devil a foot-hold. NIV

CHAPTER 13

Gift Of Discernment

Proverbs 3:21 My son, do not let wisdom and understanding out of your sight, preserve sound judgment and discretion. AMP

Discernment: the ability to judge well (in Christian contexts) perception in the absence of judgment with a view to spiritual direction and understanding.

Increase the spirit of discernment that I may know who is and is not for my life. The Holy Spirit takes over my mind and my temple so that I may discern the intention of people who come into my life. If I am uncertain about their purpose in my life then I will seek you, until I hear from you. If my ears are clouded and I am unable to hear from you LORD I ask that you remove that person from my life, and if it was your will that the person remain in my life send the HOLY SPIRIT to instruct me how to handle that person.

This is the most amazing gift you can have from GOD. I know that there are several gifts that are powerful, but this one is the MOST important one when dealing with people, but more so dating. The spirit of discernment allows you to get to know the spirit of the person that you are dating, or shall I say your potential wife or husband. It shows you that person's spiritual walk, including things about them that are unknown to man, only to GOD himself. God will reveal things to you about that person that you may get a better understanding of that person. Not all things are bad, nor good, but it plays a very important part.

For example: You notice every time that you are with this person, they seem off to you, it is something about them that you like because they seem nice, but it is something about them that makes you question their motives in your life. Some people call it intuition, I call it the spirit of the Holy Ghost speaking to you about this person. We are spirits beginning in a flesh state, and a spirit can only be abnormal for a while before it shows itself to you. Now some people can be in denial about a person for a long time because they just do not want the person they love, or a relationship with to be seen in a negative light. The Holy Spirit will lead you and guide you, to who the Father has for you. He will give you direct instructions or a personal revelation about the person. When the spirit speaks in your ear or directly to your spirit know that it is him discerning the spirit of that person.

Pray and ask GOD to increase your gift of discernment, and do not stop praying until he answers. When you get that feeling that something is not right listen to it, and when you hear that small voice say walk away, leave it alone it is the Holy Spirit working on your behalf, discerning the spirit of that person.

Every now and then we miss the mark or notice later after the relationship is over or never started that he/she was the one. And now you are confused. That is fine, go back to your prayer closet and start again, and listen. Sometimes signs will be given before destruction comes and when you pray and ask for the spirit of discernment you must know that GOD has given it unto you. It is important that you listen and if you are still confused leave it alone and leave up to GOD.

I know leaving your marriage up to GOD can be so hard when all your decisions have been with you and you are alone. When you are doing things without GOD it is hard for you to get the answers of what he has for you. To fully operate in your gift of discernment you must trust GOD because without him you are going to be lost and confused about everything. Hold your course and allow GOD to take control, Jesus to direct, and the Holy Spirit to encourage you. Before you know it, he / she will be here. This singleness is just an opportunity for GOD THE GREAT I AM to work within you.

PRAYER

Heavenly Father,

I know that I have not also walked in the spirit of discernment, and often did not know or was not aware that you had given me such an amazing gift. Today I repent for not using one of many gifts that would allow me to know who, or whom is in my presence. If I seek you and your way of doing things, increase my prayer life and meditate on your word, I will increase my gift. As I grow closer to you help me oh Lord to do amazing things in you, but more importantly help me to know how to use my gift for your kingdom, and for my life. Because of the power of Jesus, using the gift of discernment will help me avoid a lot of problems in my decision-making process.
In Jesus Name
Amen

Romans 8:6 The mind governed by flesh is death, but the mind governed by the Spirit is life and peace. NIV

CHAPTER 14

What The King Sends?

Hebrew 13:4 Have respect for marriage. Always be faithful to your partner, because GOD will punish anyone who is immoral or unfaithful in marriage. CEVUK

The LOVE that the Father has for his children is beyond what anyone can imagine. His love for you is so deep that he sent his only begotten SON to die on the cross for you Romans 3:16, so when you speak of love you must speak of the Father because he is LOVE. There are things that you will have to do in the name of LOVE whether you want to or not it is just how it goes. It should not never be anything that will cause you to step outside the will of the Father. It should never be that. Example: Wife sick cannot cook, you cook. Husband lost his job you work. It is about compromising and working with one another that your home may be blessed. It is not to divide or tear each other down. That is not love and that's not GOD's love. So, when you question or wonder "Is this person really who GOD says is for me?" Read the word LOVE and see what it means to LOVE. 1 Corinthians 13:4-7 LOVE is kind and patient, never jealous, boastful, proud, or rude. 5: Love is not selfish or quick- tempered. It does not keep a record of wrongs that others do. 6: LOVE rejoices in the truth, but not evil. 7: LOVE is always supportive, loyal, helpful, and trusting. CEVDCI

So, when you are looking to see if she is your Queen that is what you should see, if you are looking to see if he is your King that is what you should see. The world says opposite attract, but the WORD says 2 Corinthians 6:14 Do not be yoked together with unbelievers. For what do righteousness and wickedness have in common? Or what fellowship can light have with darkness. NIV

GOD always sends a replica of himself.

A FAKE replica is like a snake he will size you up, and grow to your likeness, allow you to feed him, wear him around and touch him as he pleases. Then he will hiss at you, snap at you sometimes bite you. Once he knows that you will forgive him and not get rid of him, he then will try it again, this time the bite will be to destroy you or kill you. This snake is waiting to expose you, hurt you, leave you for dead, or try to swallow you whole. Leaving you unable to return from the mental, emotional, physical, spiritual, detrimentally of his attack. His attack will have you blaming GOD for the attack, when all long it was not the real replica, but a fake replica of the KING and it is no fault of the KING, but yours. You did not realize it when you sat down to meet him/her he was not really who he/she said he was, or because you were not walking in the spirit of discernment you just ignored all the signs.

CHAPTER 14.1

The King Sends Kings

This is not hard to believe that there are still some good men in the world. God has not overlooked your struggle and pain. He will not send you someone of your past to torment you. He is an all-knowing GOD, and he knows what you need, you just must be willing to trust him in the decision-making process. GOD is the KING of all kings why in the world would he send you someone less than greatness? Oftentimes you found yourself dating a pretend KING and what you thought was the best was not at all. GOD knows that no one is perfect, so there are going to be times in your relationship that you may disagree with him and feel like he is not who GOD said he is to you, but that is normal. That teaches you to learn your KING and take time to understand him. Get to know the KING in your life and all his imperfections.

I believe sometimes GOD sends us men just like us so we can know how difficult we can be as women and when you see what you are like, know it reflects yourself which means you need to work on yourself before your KING arrives. For the most part he will be ready for you when he arrives, but the question is will you be ready for him, or will he have to wait until you get yourself together before he can enter your life. GOD will not send his KING to an unstable woman he will NOT allow you to destroy him. We as women cry and beg for a man that is nice, honest, funny, loving, kind, cute, GOD fearing man. Yet, we on the other hand are still lying, cheating, dishonesty, low key crazy, hiding anger, nasty, smart mouth, and you think GOD will send him to you? Again, I will repeat GOD knows all and he knows when you are ready for his best.

An honest man of GOD has no hidden agenda with you, he has no reason to be selling you false hope and false promises that he is unable to fulfill in the LORD. He knows his walk with GOD, and he knows his FAITH, and if he cannot handle you GOD will not send him to you. Sometimes it takes marriage to complete the promise of GOD in your life, but you must be willing NOT to settle for less than GOD's best for you. Marriage is not easy, but it is wonderful to have, when you are in GOD. When you have a marriage in GOD it does not matter what the HELL you two go through you two will remain on the promises and the word of GOD this excludes (adultery, physical abuse, mental abuse, verbal abuse, sexual abuse, spiritual abuse) Matthew 15:19 for out of the heart comes evil thoughts-murder, adultery, sexual immorality, theft, false testimony, slander. NIV

Much more is said in that scripture but when he is not in GOD those are things to expect because his heart is not right, and a man's whose heart is not in the right standing with the LORD cannot be in the right standing with a woman. Proverbs 18:22 HE who finds a wife finds what is good and receives favor from the LORD NIV.

Women STOP proposing to these men that is not biblical, and it is out of order which makes the house out of order. Again, the KING sent Kings. When you see that you must do more than the man to keep your relationship that means 1. He is not in a relationship with you or 2. He does not see you as his Favor from the LORD. You should not have to work two jobs, cook, clean, take care of the kids if any, and be intimate with him if he has not done anything in your relationship. I am not speaking of those husbands, or boyfriend who have provided and have lost their job and in between a hard spot yes, help him, but I am speaking of the one who is always in the hard spot because he never wants to do anything. He does not want to work, cook, clean, care for the kids, NOTHING at all. That is not a king but a man child. You are raising someone son all over again. That is not what you are supposed to be doing.

Kings means: the male under an independent state, especially one who inherits the position by right of birth. Revelation 17:14 These will wage war against the Lamb and the Lamb will overcome them because He is Lord of Lords and King of kings, and those who are with HIM are called and chosen and faithful. NASB

Zechariah 14:9 The LORD will be king over all the earth. On that day, the LORD will be one and his name one. NASB

Psalm 37:22 those the LORD bless will inherit the land, but those he curses will be destroy. NASB

Women choose wisely who you give that KING title to because he could be just that, a KING. But a king of who, the LORD, or himself? When your King finds you, you will know. There will be a peace in your spirit and your soul will know. But if you are unsure of him then you take him to your man or woman of GOD, if he has not already taken you to his and get Godly counsel so you two can be sure of one another. There is not a perfect relationship or marriage but there is perfection in the will of the Father. Stand strong and be of good courage and know that he that waits upon the lord shall be renewed and he will direct your path to your (soulmate) KING.

Ladies if you are dating a man who has children, and he is not involved in his kid's life, run like hell. There is no way that he is sent by the Father to parent your children if you have any and yet neglect his own. I know there are some women who are very vindictive and do not want them to be around the child, but that is what the court systems are for. Not you the court. YOU are not to be arguing with his children's mother because of what is going on between them. GOD would have worked that out before he got to you, because again the Father knows what you need, but what he needs as well.

A man that is confident in the LORD will not come to play games with your emotions, nor your mind. A man who fears, but Love GOD will not have many issues with you. He will not be insecure in your relationship, and he will never mistreat you or make you think that he is GODs gift to women instead of a gift to only you. He never takes for granted what GOD has given him, to make you regret dating again. A man of GOD is humble, honest, loving, kind and caring. He is a provider, protector, and a man of good character and integrity. He takes joy in loving you because GOD is Love and is a replica of GOD. He is slow to speak, but quick to hear, so he cares on the behalf of his family. He is submissive to the things of GOD, which is his wife, while training his children not provoking them. He dances as King David danced before the LORD because he knows that through GOD, he has you. Kings are all around you waiting to crown his Queen. Are you expecting a King or joker? Ephesians 5:28 In the same way, a husband should love his wife as much as he loves himself. A husband who loves his wife shows that he loves himself. CEVUK

PRAYER

Help me, Oh, Lord to be a woman who waits on you to send me a KING, not a pretender. Help me to lean not in my own understanding, but in all ways acknowledging you. I may want to go fast and rush into something that is not your will for me, help me to slow my pace and look for you in him, and when I cannot see a replica of you then I will walk away. I know that dating will not be easy, but if I remain humble and patient in you then you will send me my King.

In Jesus Name,

Amen

Colossians 3:19 A husband must love his wife not abuse her. CEV

CHAPTER 14.2

The King Sends Queens

Yes, Kings GOD has prepared that special lady for you. Not every woman is broken, damaged, and angry at men. Not every woman wants to damage you, break you down and make you feel the rafts of her ex's. There are some women that are waiting patiently for you to crown her as your wife. Men you have played house for so long with so many women that were not your wife that you lost hope and thought it would be better to have friends and some with benefits. That is not the plan for you from the Father.

Men you must be mindful when you are dating and looking for someone to share your last name make sure you are ready for that commitment. GOD will not send you his precious jewel for you to destroy her. Proverbs 12:4 A helpful wife is a jewel for her husband, but a shameful wife will make his bones rot. CEV

You must know who carries your last name, because you are stuck with this one for the rest of your life. GOD never intended for divorce unless one has been unfaithful in marriage. So, when you take on those vows you take on a commitment not just to her, but GOD and openly to your family, friends, and other females. That is why the vows are spoken aloud so you and her can hear them and take them to heart.

Men you must be mindful that every beautiful woman that you meet does not mean that is who you eat with, sleep, playhouse, and spend your money with. You must understand the importance of a wife and she cannot just be anybody. She needs you as much as you need her, and you must be willing and open to her. GOD knows the type of woman that you need in your life as well as your kids if you have any. GOD will not send you an insecure woman, that will verbally, emotionally, physically abuse, or financially abuse you in any type of way.

GOD knows and understands that you need a woman that is honest, faithful, supportive, encouraging, and understanding. GOD will never take away the things you need as a man to be what he calls you to be in him, and sometimes a bride's help brings the best out of you. You will always need GOD, but a wife is a bonus to you, that's GOD FAVOR unto you. That goes to show you how GOD views marriages, but how he views a wife as well to you. Never take for granted the person GOD sends in your life to be what you need her to be to you, but more so what you need to be to her. GOD takes good pride in creating her for you, so embrace every moment with her. Do not take any woman and do not settle for any woman, but GOD's best.

Sometimes holding onto past relationships can hold you back from loving your GOD sent woman, and sometimes going through the wrong relationships help groom you for the right relationship when you have an open heart and willingness to love again. GOD takes every tear you cried inwards as well as outward. He will take your brokenness from past relationships and crown KING for the right QUEEN.

You should not have to argue every day with a woman, fuss with her, beg her to believe you, bend over backwards to please her, always having to compromise to make her happy while you are unhappy. Proverbs 21:19 It is better to be in the desert than at home with a nagging, complaining wife. CEVUK

Marriage is a compromising relationship and the both of you should be willing to compromise for one another because you two love each other. Ephesians 5:22 A wife should put her husband first, as she does the LORD. CEVUK

You should NEVER have to choose between your wife and your kids. If you are involved with a woman who does not want you to be involved in your children's life, she means you no good, and that is not your Queen. Once they are adults that could change, but as little kids they need both parents, and because you are adding someone else to their life that makes it more the merrier to the child to have double the blessing of your wife. If she treats your children differently from her own or differently then you may have to question her motives for your life. Not every woman is meant to be parents to another woman's children and that's fine too, GOD knows best, and he knows if you have children who to send you too.

Proverbs 14:1 A woman's family is held together by her wisdom, but it can be destroyed by her foolishness. CEVUK

Take your time to get to know your wife. Date her as much as possible that you two may have an understanding about one another in the relationship. Take her out, and sometimes allow her to take you out to show that she appreciates you for being in her life as well. A woman has her heart open to love a man, and sometimes it could be the wrong man, but she is willing to love, again. Allow her to love you as you love her like CHRIST loved the church. Never look at her less than what she is to you. She is your Ruth as you are her Boaz.

PRAYER

Lord,

I have not always been honest with women with my expectations as a man and allowed them to make decisions that I was not comfortable with and did not really desire to do from the beginning, it was only to please her. GOD help me to be the man that I need to be for my wife, but more so help me to choose the RIGHT wife for my life. I cannot make this decision alone and I fear that I may ruin someone else's wife if I choose the wrong wife. You said she is FAVOR unto me so send my FAVOR unto me. As I prepare my life for her, also prepare her life for me.

In Jesus Name,
Amen

Proverbs 18:22 A man's greatest treasure is his wife; she is a gift from the LORD. CEVUK

CHAPTER 15

Be Open

Songs of Solomon 3:1 All night long on my bed I looked for the one my heart loves. I looked for him but did not find him. NIV

You must be willing to be open to GOD, let him pick your mate, because he knows what you need and not what you want. Sometimes your wants can cause more pain than happiness. You want to be happy with your mate, but you should want two the other one being Christ. And if he/she is not in Christ it would be hard to please you. One would say you could have a pretty good relationship without GOD, but it will not last long if it is not ordained by GOD himself. You can have all your heart desires if your desire is that GOD hand pick your mate.

It can be hard picking the right person to be your wife or your husband when making the decision yourself, but when GOD picks him/ her it is like a perfect pair of shoes that fits very well and is comfortable on your feet. When you grow out that size you get another pair just like that if not better. Your relationship will fit perfectly at the beginning and will be very pleased, but as you too grow to know one another your relationship should grow into another level.

I cannot tell you what a perfect mate is but, I can tell you this if you put your trust in the Father, he will direct your path and order your steps for the perfect mate for you. No one is perfect, but he/

she will be perfect for you to say I DO. GOD never gives you something that you expect, but he always sends the unexpected because he knows what you need. Your wants should never overpower what you need in your life, or your children (if applies) lives.

You spend your time running behind you are want, praying for your need, yet missing who GOD has for you. Open your heart to love beyond your expectations and watch GOD bless you with a mate that will love you as Christ loves the church. Take your time and date outside of what you are used to. GOD is love, love conquers all and he who must love you may not be the same race. It may be different at first just as anything but if you are open and willing to love, he/she will love you as GOD does. He/ She will love GOD just as much as you do and would make you happier than you could imagine. We are all created in his image and likeness, but we are not always open to loving others outside of our nationality. 1 Corinthians 11:11 As far as the Lord is concerned, men and women need each other. CEVUK

GOD chooses your mate, not you when he is creating him or her. He is not looking at their skin color, their culture, their environment, their heritage, but their heart. LOVE does not see those things it just sees LOVE. We are all from the same bloodline of JESUS CHRIST. Our color, culture, environment, heritage is the descent of Abraham the Father of many nations.

GOD said I would never send hatred to your door, I would never send someone who hates your culture, your heritage, your children, your color. I would NEVER send someone that would hate you. That is including their family and friends, and if anyone HATE you two, they also HATE me.

We must get out of the customs, and tradition of who our spouses are, and who he or she supposed to be. GOD himself has created us all. To know GOD is a powerful thing, to never say that we could marry outside of our custom he said not to adapt to their ways, worshiping idols, and put no GOD before me and living immoral. Living any other way outside of his will is a no. If your spouse is not in the word of GOD and you are questioning yourself and think he or she is a replica of CHRIST, and if the answer is NO then you know what that means. He or She is not the one he has chosen for you, but you have chosen him or her for yourself. Be opened to love him/her that is new to the kingdom of Christ but is seeking him as well. We were all once lost at one point of time. Please be wise and know that you cannot counsel them. You can lead them, and guide them to Christ, and allow GOD to do the rest.

PRAYER

God,

I know that I have made it difficult for you to send my mate to me, and I repent for asking you for what I want instead of what I need. Take this list that I have created in my heart and remove it and replace it with what you want Oh, GOD. Cleanse me from the desire of my expectations and create in me a new heart that I can love as you love but be open to whomever you have created for me. I know you love me, and you have nothing but the best for me so as I wait patiently for you. Help me to be open to receive who you have for me. Although my heart desires (state the name) and your word say that you will give me the desires of my heart. Help me Oh LORD because my heart can cause confusion to help me to be open to my husband/ wife that you have chosen for me. You know who I need for my life, my children (if applies), and ministry. I have never truly experienced true love. Please give me a person whose will is to be obedient to you, and your word and love me as you love me and my children (if applies).

In Jesus Name
Amen

Isaiah 11:3 He will delight in obeying the LORD. He will not judge by appearance nor make a decision based on hearsay. NLT

CHAPTER 16

God's Timing

Ecclesiastes 3:7 A time to tear and a time to mend, a time to be silent and a time to speak. NIV

Timing is everything with GOD, he never seems to amaze me with his timing. He has a time that will never equal up to our timing. Our Father does not work on a 24 hour a day schedule or 7 days a week. He works as he sees fit, but it is always on his time. We have all the time in the world to wait on a man or woman to get their life together, but we do not have time for GOD to send that special someone for us. We act as if it is taking a lifetime to get married, but there are things that you must do before GOD can release you to your spouse, and that is the reason why you are not married.

Timing is crucial to your marriage; you must be right before your spouse comes into your life. You can move too fast into a relationship and marry someone premature and you can find yourself divorced. You must know that GOD has your best interest in heart, and he would never send you unprepared to your spouse let alone send him/ her unprepared to you. During your wait time let that be GODs timing to work on you for his glory and for his ministry. GOD has greater thing he wants to use you for in ministry not just for marriage. Marriage alone is a ministry and if you are unable and willing to be submissive to GOD, then in your marriage you will not be ready for marriage.

With GOD's timing comes preparation for him to bring forth the best spouse you can be to your mate. GOD must make sure you are the best when sending you, and that you are healed, and delivered from any past relationships that would hinder this marriage. GOD is a GOD of order and he does everything decent and in order. So, it would be out of order for him to send an unprepared mate to a prepared mate. It would be out of order for you as a woman on one knee asking a man to marry you. It is out of order if you are asking GOD to honor you shacking up until you two say I do. It would be out of order for him to allow the two of you to get married and neither of you have spiritual counseling or any type of counseling. Some may agree that it is needed, and some may not agree, but it is needed.

Within his timing he makes sure all that is done before he makes you the one with another. In his timing he sees how you care for yourself before he sends you or sends your mate. If you do not love yourself and mistreat yourself, he will not send you someone to mistreat as well. Because you two become one. GODs timing will never match your timing, but he is always on time.

You know you want a husband or wife. You're ready to say yes, but GOD said "no, there are some other things that I have to strengthen you in ministry before I can release him/her to you". He must know that when you are married you will not stop prayer, coming to church, tithing, ministry. He must know that you are sold out to him whether he/she comes, leaves, or stays. You will remain faithful unto him. Why would GOD send you a person if you're not ready? He gives us the desires of our heart and because you desire him/her and he gives it to you does not mean you are ready for it and when things get out of control, you are like Adam blaming Eve for this woman you gave unto me.

FAQ's

Q: Should I wait for my husband or wife?
A: Yes, while still working in ministry.

Q: Do I have to give up dating?
A: You should know that you are hearing GOD clearly on who your spouse is and that you are not rushing into someone that is not in the will of GOD.

Q: How long do I hold on to the hope of getting married?
A: Until GOD sends him or her. You must practice patience. Patience brings on a lot of rewards when you are waiting for GOD and not yourself to make it happen.

Q: DO I have to be saved to be married?
A: No, but if you want your marriage to truly be honored by GOD it is important that you make the necessary steps to be saved.

In GODs timing he will be able to lead you, guide you and direct your path to the right person for your life, and the lives of your kids.

PRAYER

Heavenly Father,

Your timing is always better than mine. Although I think I am ready for who you have for me, you always show me that I am not ready. Father help me to be strong and stand on you by selecting my mate. Help me to be strong in you and not myself rushing through the process and causing so much destruction because I think my time outweigh yours. Because I know you give me the desires of my heart and it is my heart to be married now and meet my husband or wife. Let your will be done so I may choose you for me and not who I think you have for me because I am waiting on you. GOD, I know it is time for everything, but let everything be in your timing.

In Jesus Name

Amen

Ecclesiastes 3:8 A time to love and a time to hate, a time for war and a time for peace. KJV

CHAPTER 17

Don't Force It

Psalm 55:11 Destructive forces are at work in the city, threats and lies never leave its streets. NIV

This scripture may not have made sense with this topic of this book on relationship, and it did not make sense with this chapter, but it worked itself into my message, with what I believe GOD was trying to relay. When you are in a forced relationship it can bring destruction, threats, lies, and mental damage in your life, never leaving your mind, but lingering in your thoughts. It all becomes a part of you because you have taken on a relationship that was never meant to be. For some reason you find yourself thinking and believing that the relationship will get better if you hold on little while longer you call that (FAITH), or if you change then the person will change. Maybe if we get married or have a child together it would get better. Deep down you knew that person would never change, and the relationship would never work itself out, but you could not imagine yourself without that person.

A forced relationship is like forcing a pair of small shoes on your feet, you probably could get away with it the first few hours or maybe the first few days because you are believing you are breaking the shoes to fit your feet, in some cases you must. But after a while of wearing the shoes, you notice that your feet continue to hurt, and the light bulb finally comes on in your head that it is not your feet it is the shoe size that does not feel right.

That is how relationships sometimes start off. They start off tight because of two different people trying to find a common ground with one another and comparing one another to past relationships. Hoping for the best and believing that it would get better once they get to know one another some more. Months roll around then turn into a year and you still find yourself in that uncomfortable situation. In your mind you believe it is going to get better. You start praying and believing GOD to work out the relationship, but it is not getting better it is getting worse than it was before. You begin to make excuses for why things have not changed, and you stop praying and believing for a change and start trusting the process of you two. The whole time GOD is showing you DESTRUCTION is about to take place if you do not leave the situation. You believe that destruction cannot come to your home because "GOD ordained this relationship". In the mist you find yourself losing, joy, peace, hope, faith, love, your house, car, your respect, and your kids. You are now unable to go to work because of your stress, depression, sickness.

The relationship was never meant to be, and GOD is trying to warn you before the signs get bigger than what you can handle. Now with your ignoring the signs with what you have lost you still do not believe it has anything to do with the relationship, so you stay. Now you are picking up depression, lust, anger, bitterness, hatred, and sickness because your body cannot deal with the stress of the relationship and every time he or she THREATENS to leave, you cannot imagine yourself without that person. So, you go over and beyond to keep them happy pleasing them and yet your still unhappy. Now you are questioning whether everything that person told you was a LIE or was it just something that he/ she was saying to keep you and now you do not believe anything they do or say to be from a place of truth and love. It is not to say that this person did not love you or never loved you, they just cannot be what you need them to be because he/ she was never meant to be your spouse. Now their character and their integrity are questionable to you, but you have now been in this relationship for years. In the beginning when the relationship was new

82

you ignored the tightness. Then during the six-month stage when GOD was showing you the signs, while you still had your joy, peace, happiness, love, and sound mind to leave, you kept forcing it to fit because he/ she "loved me", or "I loved them", and "it's going to get better", and "change comes with every relationship".

Change that comes with more pain than joy is not that kind of change you should have. When your relationship of any kind starts changing for the worse you know it is time for you to go no matter what that person says or how much you love them. GOD always has better than what you think is good. Change will come in any relationship, but it is always for the better, to build each other and help them to become better for the kingdom, for you, for themselves, for your family. Change should never cause you to contemplate suicide, become depressed, an alcoholic or abuse any substance as an outlet to be released from the stress of the relationship.

Those are the signs of a FORCED RELATIONSHIP. If you are a person who loves GOD or getting to know GOD, then you know or learn how GOD is a gentleman. He will never force himself upon you and will allow you to receive him in your timing. When you are in a relationship where you must force yourself into happiness then it is not GOD, but it is all you. But it goes back to my earlier chapter when I spoke on GODLY counsel if you have a pastor or elder you can trust they will know how to pray you through this relationship, but you must trust GOD through the whole process.

You may have been in the relationship for so long you may not see anything wrong with it or think it is normal but normal is not normal in a force relationship. Normal is when two can communicate, share opinions without feeling less than the other person. Normal is sharing your goals and dreams and helping each other achieve them. Normal is NOT cursing each other out, normal is laughing until you cry. Normal is NOT crying because he/ she left or cheated, normal is having that friend you can turn to, when you have no other person that is normal. This may sound like a perfect relationship and it is when it is not forced but ordained by GOD. There will be times where you two will disagree, but it will not be to destroy one another. You can agree to disagree.

These are some questions you may have:

Q: How will I know if my relationship is ordained by GOD?
A: I told you before GOD only sends a replica of himself. Although he or she may have bad days, good days etc. GOD has emotion as well.

> Number 32:10 The LORD's anger was aroused that day and he swore this other because they have not followed me wholeheartedly, not one of those who were twenty years old or more when they came out of Egypt will see the land I promised on oath to Abraham, Isaac, and Jacob. NIV

> John 3:16 GOD so loved the world he gave his one and only Son, that whoever believes in him shall not perish but have eternal life. NIV

> Galatians 5:22 But the fruit of the Spirit is love, joy, peace, forbearance, kindness, goodness, faithfulness. NIV

Those are a few scriptures of GOD expressing his emotions and it is more than that. These are just a few to let you know that he or she will express different emotions, but the emotions should never be to the point of bringing destruction to you or questioning who they are to you. If what they are saying to you is truthful or lies. The sad, but important part is IT NEVER LEAVES THE STREET, the street of your mind, the words, and actions of someone from a forced relationship will leave you with mental issues. It causes so much damage to your mental state that your mind will never receive someone other than that person. It causes you to deal with people in a different manner. It causes you to deal with people who have never had any bad intentions for you, but to love you, be with you, care for you, and support you. And because your mind is infatuated with the forced relationship, you see no true happiness in any other relationship. A forced relationship would have you acting as if you are still in a relationship with that person after the relationship is long over. Once you leave a forced relationship it is hard for you to express happiness without fear of that person saying something causing you to regret being happy. It will have you still catering to them when you are in their presence. Physically you know you are not in a relationship, but mentally it is something about that person that has your whole demeanor change when you are in their presence.

When he left for the last time, he did not know what he was doing, but GOD did, and with that move came a change and renewed mind in him CHRIST JESUS. If GOD had to give up his son for me, who am I not to give up a man for him? The same applies to you.

PRAYER

Oh! God,

I know that sometimes I do not always wait upon you, to do what you need to do in my life. I do things my way, and when I do that it causes a forced relationship to happen that is not pleasing unto you. GOD, please forgive me for forcing a relationship that you had no intention that I be involved in, that I created myself. As I wait for you to send my husband/wife cleanse me from any mental, spiritual, emotional, or physical forced relationship that I may NOT be aware of and unaware of from any person.

In Jesus Name I Pray
Amen

Psalm 51:2 Wash me thoroughly from my wickedness and guilt and cleanse me from my sin. AMP

CHAPTER 18

S.h.a.c.k.i.n.g Up

1 Corinthians 7:9 if they do not have sufficient
self-control, they should marry; for it is better
to marry than to burn with passion. AMP

Shacking is the easiest thing to do when you are in a "committed" relationship with someone. It is so much easier for us to
live with a person than to marry a person. I never really understood that concept, but I was guilty of shacking up before marriage.
Many reasons are to see how we get along in the same house before
we get married. For some we never made it to the altar. That is a
shame. We did all of that and still did not make it to the altar. I
believe the Holy Spirit will convict us, but we will ignore it. I am
not saying that shacking up before marriage does not mean you two
would not get married, but what I am saying is that we must honor
GOD in all that we do. We cannot pick and choose which part of the
bible, or the word of GOD we want to follow. I cannot change the
word, but I can enlighten you on it.

The truth of the matter is in my old way of thinking I thought
it was the most amazing thing in the world, to be living with a person that you want to spend the rest of your life with. I am thinking building a home, cooking for him, washing/ ironing his clothes,
and maintaining a clean house for him he would see that I am wife
material. I did those things for my children as well, but he was the

provider, he was the head of the house. He was who I would submit to and ask for his opinions and thoughts on decisions making in the house. Thinking since we are going to be married soon might as well start practicing. Practicing something that may not happen is not good and it is not pleasing to GOD. I cannot take away anyone wanting to spend all their time with their mate, until marriage but if you are holding yourself until marriage shacking up only causes temptation and will eventually cause you to fall.

This is a touchy topic because everybody has their opinion about what is right and what is wrong. Everyone is mature enough and they can do what works for them. Who am I to judge? I too was in a stay of repentance with GOD until I made up in my mind that I would surrender my life to him and live the most HOLY life as possible. Where I fell, he would help me, and when I am weak, he will be my strength.

> 2 Samuel 22:33 GOD is my strong fortress; he sets the blameless in HIS way. When you are taught the word of GOD and you refuse to listen there are consequences for your actions. AMP

> James 4:17 If anyone, then, knows the good they ought to do and does not do it, it is sin for them. NIV

Society and some of our family has taught us that it was alright that we can have sex before marriage, we could live with whomever we wanted to, and we could do as we please. GOD has given us free will. Some may have told you that there will be consequences for your actions but never knew what the consequences would be. We may have done it anyhow, and some of us may have felt our consequences then, and some of us may be living with our consequences now. For some of us, our consequences have not caught up to us yet, but when it does, we will pay for it. GOD will judge everyone according to his word, and we must answer for our actions. We can cry that we did not know, but you knew that GOD was real and as soon as you started believing in him, you should have begun to pick up the book about him to teach him as your FATHER. Everybody loves GOD the provider, healer. He is your sugar daddy handing out blessings. Not every blessing you think you got came from him. Some came from the other master you serve.

Shacking-up can delay some things for you and hold up the process to where GOD is trying to take you. So, who he is trying to bring in your life? Sometimes we hold on to these relationships because we are in a lease with someone. You find yourself miserable, no longer happy as you were in the beginning of the relationship. The passion you had you no longer have. The habits that person has is the most annoying thing to you. You soon learn that what you saw when you were dating is not the same person now living in the home, and it is like dating two different people.

When you are praying and asking GOD to bless your home or when you are living with someone and not married, it binds GOD hands to bless you. GOD does everything decently and in order. **1 Corinthians 14:40 Do everything properly and in order. CEVUK**

First start coming to church. Show that you can provide and lead our family. <u>Living together before marriage would cause us to have sex before marriage, along with a cursed house. Living with no order.</u>

Take a leap of faith to walk away from his/her and their foolishness to be his wife/ her husband. Now I know that will be hard for some of you to do, because you have been there for so many years. Please understand if you are operating in ministry, and you are believing in GOD and his word, then you must grow and be mature to GOD's way. I was once told why buy the cow when you can have the milk for free? My FREEDOM came with a price, and it was not free, so why should anyone else have me for free. We could take that chance by giving up all GOD has restored in us for a pretend marriage. Remember you are not a pretend person so pretend marriage you will not partake in.

When GOD gave me this topic, he reminded me that SHACKIN UP is only a person's way to Stay in the Home until he/ she decides to Acknowledge to CHRIST that he's King and in himself/herself Nothing is Going to happen because it is an Unfilled Promise. In man nothing is possible but in GOD all things are possible. Luke 1:37 Nothing is impossible for GOD. CEVUK

I know first-hand sometimes it is hard to maintain a home alone, and having more bills than money, and even harder with children. Not to mention the nights when you are alone just wishing that someone was with you and thinking about all the things you two could do or would do if you lived together. He/ She could cook while you wash clothes or pick the kids up while you go to the grocery store. And living with a mate is sometimes convenient for the both of you, but it is something about trusting GOD, that he has got you and you never have to worry about anything. Lonely pray, horny pray, broke pray, lost pray. Praying breaks yokes and bondage and while you are seeking your FATHER, he is seeking your spouse on your behalf that would be just as effective in your two marriages than you.

GOD,

I have lived my life doing things my own way, I have stayed with men/women and have played house for a long time. Sometimes I did not know how I was going to live without this person or pay my bills or take care of my (our) children without us living together. That showed me that I had little faith in you and did not believe that you were able to see me through this place. These nights are lonely, and the companionship is real in my life. I need someone who will wait for me and build in the kingdom with me and share in ministry. GOD does not need someone who needs a home, and I do not want to be with someone for any reason that is your reason GOD.

Help me to be strong and patient.

In Jesus Name, Amen

Psalms 119:114 You are my place of safety and my shield. Your word is my only hope. CEV

FINAL NOTE TO READER

I don't claim to be an expert on love and relationships, but I do claim to know the FATHER and how he operates. This book was not written to commend anyone, or cause shame or hurt to any one life. It is to open your eyes as mine have been open. I have lived for many men, and for everyone else. But to live for GOD is another level and new experience. In this process I lost a lot, but I never lost my hope nor my FAITH in the LORD this book only caused me to LOVE and TRUST him more. Why? Because he went out of his way to show me why he was not ready for me to date, and that I need to know and understand how he operates in my life. I have operated in my own way of things for so long that he was not going to keep allowing me to make the same bad judgements on men, and relationships.

There are no perfect relationships and that is good, but all bad relationships had lessons that I had to learn from. Once I opened my eyes to see, my ears to listen, and my heart to learn the true meaning of LOVE. GOD was ready to teach and show me some things. LOVE is an action and until you take the first action in your life with LOVING yourself how can you LOVE someone else, and what you think is LOVE really is not its LUST. Know that you have a true understanding of GOD and his way of LOVE. You can move out the way and let him send you that REAL LOVE, GOD's LOVE.

When GOD wanted me to change the title of this book it really didn't make sense to me, and I couldn't figure out for the life of me how he wanted me to relate this message to the public, but as he began to minister to me he was telling me that, if lies and deceit could cause the minds of people who truly desire to love and to be loved than his love could go beyond that and be so much more. You must be ready to love and to be loved in return before he could bring anyone in your life.

LIE: is an intentionally false statement.

DECEIT: the action or practice of deceiving someone by concealing or misrepresenting the truth.

When you understand the truth about dating, you start doing things differently than how you would normally do things but more so when you understand that LIES & DECEIT come when you are not willing to. Acknowledge your faults. You are always playing the victim, not willing to Get ROOTED in the word of GOD to know the truth about relationship. You are not taking the time to renew your Mind but allowing your Matter to make decisions and still seeing yourself how other people see you instead of Knowing how GOD sees you. If you think your Damaged goods, GOD recognizes that your still good. You are willing to take the time to learn someone else's value but will not Learn your self-worth so that you can be Free from yourself, take time to HEAL, and get to know yourself.

You're so wrapped up in LIES & DECEIT that you are not open to who GOD could be sending to be a blessing or being open to GOD's Timing for your mate. You're still forcing what GOD does not want you to Force, believing that your relationship works better when you were SHACKING UP. When you are willing to go back after seeing that pattern never changed from that person to a new person, you ignore the gift that was given to you. Free Discernment gives you the foresight to see when the King sends your King or Queen.

God,

I may not know everything about relationships, nor do everything right in a relationship that will please you. GOD you gave me some guidelines, to start seeking you` for my personal life. After reading this book I understand your words and what you are telling me to do but help me Oh! Lord that I May live a life pleasing unto you while I am waiting or dating.

In Jesus Name
Amen

> 2 Corinthians 5:17 Therefore if any person is [in grafted] in Christ (the Messiah) he is a new creation (a new creature altogether); the old [previous moral and spiritual condition] has passed away. Behold, the fresh and new has come! AMPC

Message to You:

Keeping yourself sometimes seems to be the most difficult process after salvation because you are so used to doing and being with whomever your flesh desires. The desires of the flesh will open so many doors that you could lose sight of who you are in GOD, and who you are

destined and created to be in Him. GOD has chosen you to be an open vessel for him, that He may use you as a witness unto his people. GOD cannot fully use you when everyone else is using you too. It is impossible to mix darkness with light.

Luke 16:13 No one can serve two masters, for you will hate one and love the other; you will be devoted to one and despise the other. You cannot serve God and be enslaved to money. NLT

That same scripture applies to everything including your flesh.

As believers we want to please GOD, but sometimes our flesh tries to please two masters. We cannot fully serve GOD if you do not fully surrender your whole body, mind, and soul. Not just your hands and feet, but your whole body. Living this Christian life takes much discipline, but it will be worth it in the end.

I believe that during the process of me writing this book, GOD has been teaching me how to live a Holy life and to remain